XXX SEX TALES

EXPLICIT DIRTY EROTICA SHORT STORIES

SHON GACY,STERLING KLEMM, JULI
MATESON, BLANCA CRANSTON, CANDRA
AUBREY

plicit Press

CHAPTER 1

"RAVENOUS"

KIEL AND BAYLEE SIONN were on their way from Lawrence to Topeka when their car broke down along a deserted stretch of Kansas highway. Well, it wasn't exactly a highway per se, more like an exit that Kiel never should've taken. Now, the couple sat in their mid-sized sedan looking at their dead cell phones and arguing about what they were going to do next.

"If we just wait, our phones will charge and we can call a tow truck," twenty-nine-year-old Kiel ran a hand through his russet curls, completely frustrated with himself. His dark gray eyes turned towards his twenty-seven-year-old wife. She'd pulled her legs up onto her seat, curling them beneath her. With her short sandy locks and cherubic face, she looked more like a high school senior than a married mother of four-year-old twins. Fortunately, for this trip, the kids were with grandma.

"That's if the car battery isn't dead and if we can even get a signal," her obsidian eyes sparked.

·   ·   ·

Her temper had always been easy to turn to passion, but Kiel wasn't sure it'd work this time.

Kiel opened his mouth to say something – just what he wasn't sure – but stopped when he saw the flash of metal in the rearview mirror. When he pointed it out to Baylee, she grinned and climbed out of the car. Kiel got followed, an uneasy feeling in his stomach. Baylee came around the front of the car and leaned against his door, the half-grin on her face telling him that she was well aware of the picture she painted. Tight jean cut-off shorts that ended just below her ass cheeks and a form-fitting tank top that left a strip of her tanned stomach bare. And he was fairly sure she wasn't wearing a bra.

"Car problems?" The driver of the pick-up was tall and lean with ebony curls and baby blue eyes that instantly darkened when they saw Baylee.

"Got a cell phone?" Kiel spoke up.

"They don't work out here," the young man glanced back at the other person in the truck. "Would you mind driving us to a phone or maybe a tow truck?" Kiel watched the passenger

walk towards them. He was a few inches taller than the driver, muscles clearly defined under a tight t-shirt. Corn silk blond hair danced in the breeze and eyes the color of the midnight sky completed the package.

"I have a better idea," Baylee stretched her arms up, revealing more skin. "Why don't you two gentlemen give my husband here the keys to your truck and you wait here with me?"

The dark-haired stranger wasted no time bending Baylee over the hood of the car. Surprising her, he dropped to his knees, tugging down her shorts. He whistled as he exposed the smooth tanned skin of her ass – and her total lack of panties.

"Look at that," he ran his finger between Baylee's folds and she shivered. "Damn, she's even

wet."

Baylee cried out as the dark-haired man buried his face between her thighs, shoving her legs further apart. As his tongue burrowed into her pussy, the blonde leaned over her, ripping the back of her tank top. He ignored her protests, half-hearted as they were, and maneuvered her out of the ruined garment, groping at her small breasts before letting her fall back against the hood.

"Fuck me, please," she pleaded, writhing on her car. When the blonde pulled both hands behind her back and tied her wrists with her shirt, she moaned.

The dark-haired man stood, face glistening with her juices, and pulled a foil packet from his pocket. The blonde watched, arms crossed over his massive chest, as his friend rolled on the condom. Seconds later, Baylee wailed as the dark-haired man plunged his cock into her pussy. He pounded into her, each jerk of his hips eliciting a series of sharp cries. He grabbed her bound hands, pulling her arms up at an almost painful angle. As he yanked her upper body off the hood of the car, Baylee's body began to quake, knees buckling.

"Fuck, her pussy's shaking all around me," the dark-haired man gasped out, hips losing their rhythm. He came with a loud, drawn-out groan, ass flexing.

Baylee's body collapsed on the hood as the stranger pulled out, sweat-sticky skin keeping her from sliding off. She had no time to recover or to even process. The blonde already had his cock out, condom on and, as soon as his friend moved away, he grabbed Baylee and flipped her. Before she'd fully come to rest on her back, the blonde took hold of her slim hips and slammed all ten inches into her.

Baylee screamed, back arching as he filled her. The blonde's teeth clenched, muscles rippling under golden skin as he set a brutal pace, driving the air from Baylee's lungs and turning her screams into a soundless expulsion of air. He bent forward, not losing a single stroke, and opened his mouth wide to take almost an entire breast inside. Her lithe body trembled, convulsed, under the assault until, suddenly, her eyes rolled back in her head and her limbs went limp. And still, the blonde rode her body, mouth leaving dark marks all along her tanned flesh.

"When I came to, the dark-haired guy was doing me again," Baylee snuggled up against her husband's side, hand lightly caressing the obvious erection tenting Kiel's pants. "Wait till you see what comes next. It's fucking hot."

Kiel kept his eyes on the television screen where his wife was being manhandled onto the ground to sit astride a dark-haired stranger. He had a feeling he knew what was coming next. After all, he'd seen her swollen, red hole when he'd returned with the men's pick-up. His dick twitched under Baylee's hands. His own hands were also busy, one under her shirt, fondling her breasts, the other down the front of her pants, lightly stroking her swollen clit. Every time he touched a particularly sensitive piece of flesh, her breathing hitched and a jolt of desire went straight through him.

"That new camera is amazing," Kiel said, brushing his lips against her temple. "Maybe next time we can figure out how to get some hand-held shots to go with the ones from the tripod."

"As long as you find me more guys like that," Baylee's hand slid under Kiel's waistband and took him in hand. "I'm game." She wiggled against him, squeezing his rock-hard cock. "Now, let's fuck."

"You're one hungry woman," Kiel moaned. She hissed into his ear. "Ravenous."

CHAPTER 2

A DATE WITH MR. RIGHT

LINDSEY HAD BEEN WAITING for days for her date with Danny. And now it was finally happening. Danny had arranged a nice romantic picnic for them, near a waterfall. Lindsey couldn't help but be thankful for taking time off from work to go to Antigua. It was there that she'd met Danny. And now, she believed that he was truly the man that could complete her. It felt amazing being loved, especially when her lover looked so damn good.

Physically speaking Danny was a very attractive man. He rose to about six foot two inches, and easily towered over her petite frame. He had a tanned golden brown complexion that always left her wishing she could get a tan like him. He also had a gorgeous smile; Danny could light up an entire room with just his smile. His set of pearly white teeth and his dimpled chin complimented his good looks perfectly.

. . .

As they sat on the grass, Lindsey looked out at the waterfall with admiration in her eyes.

She had finished her sandwich and was listening to Danny, watching his profile as he gazed at the waterfall crashing into the rocks. She sighed; Danny turned to look at her.

"And how was your lunch, love?"

Lindsey smiled. "Amazing. Wonderful. I've never had such delicious food. I feel like I'm repeating myself, but truly I cannot remember when I've enjoyed such great food. Or such great company." She set her beer aside, reaching up to touch Danny's cheek.

Danny took her hand, kissing her fingers. He pushed her down on the blanket, covering her body with his. "We cannot swim for one hour after eating. What shall we do in that hour, Lindsey?" He captured her mouth with his, biting her lower lip softly, his tongue flicking over her mouth.

Lindsey could feel her body react to his kisses and the latent promise of his words. "Should I take you here, on the blanket?"

Lindsey nodded and before she could speak, Danny covered her mouth again with his. He was more forceful than before, seeming to want her now, all languid foreplay gone, replaced by a primal desire. Lindsey was ready to meet him fully, ready to be taken, and take.

She sat up, pulling her dress over her head. Danny worked his trunks down over his well-muscled legs, his erection popping free. She took him in her hand, stroking his cock, feeling him shudder beneath her touch. It was a powerful feeling to be regarded as an equal, Lindsey discovered, and not someone to be dominated during sex.

Danny reached between her legs, running his fingers over her pussy, thrusting two fingers inside her, searching for that sweet spot while rubbing the heel of his hand over her swollen clit. The friction of his hand against her clit combined with his thrusting fingers was incredible. She could feel herself convulsing at each thrust, feel herself grow wetter by the moment. She pushed herself hard against him, suddenly aching for him to fill her with his cock.

"Fuck me, Danny, take me now. Fuck me hard." Lindsey heard herself say the words before she realized what she had uttered. But once she heard them, she felt powerful and in control. And deliciously dirty.

"All right, Lindsey. You ask, and you shall receive." Lindsey felt Danny take his hand away and then felt the head of his cock sliding against her wet pussy. He held himself briefly and then thrust into her hard, exhaling a loud moan, stretching her, filling her completely. She gasped as he pulled back slowly and thrust hard into her again, burying himself to the hilt in her. He set a fast pace, pounding into her over and over and lying claim to her pussy with his cock.

Lindsey drew her legs up as Danny shifted position slightly, setting her calves on his shoulders. What she gave up in control of her movements she gained in penetration. She felt as if Danny's cock reached all the way to her ribcage, each thrust echoing throughout her body.

Danny held himself above her body, braced on his hands, looking down at Lindsey. She ran her hands up his corded arms, feeling the solid muscle beneath the smooth skin. She looked down, able to see his cock sliding in and out of her, watching it glistening with her juices.

"Lindsey....oh, love, you are so beautiful when you're being fucked, especially when I'm fucking you." Danny's dark eyes were watching her. Lindsey's eyes widened; she was not used to hearing those words. She had no idea what to say in response but didn't think a response was strictly necessary.

Danny picked up the pace, even more, slamming into her hard with each thrust, moaning loudly now. She felt herself being pushed up the blanket by the force of his thrusts, her sunburned skin adding a delicious tingle of pain as a counterpoint to his delicious fucking.

Suddenly, Danny cried out, thrusting into her with several sharp thrusts, his cock throbbing and twitching as he pumped his load into her waiting pussy. Lindsey watched him grimace, a look of mixed pain and pleasure, as his orgasm continued, his mouth open in a silent cry. He held himself inside her, slowly relaxing as his orgasm faded.

"Sorry, love. That one just came out of nowhere. You have that effect on me, I guess." He winced as he pulled out of her, lying on his back beside her on the blanket, throwing his arm over his eyes. She watched him, laying in the sun, his semi-erect cock resting on his thigh, wet and glistening with their combined juices. Lindsey sighed, sitting up on the blanket. Danny reached over without taking his arm from his eyes, idly rubbing Lindsey's leg, trailing his fingers up her inner thigh.

"We need to take care of you though; you must be a bit frustrated at the moment. Can't let you be short-changed. That wouldn't be good island hospitality."

CHAPTER 3

MY NYMPHOMANIA FUCK STATS

I HEARD the statistic over the radio after showering and drying my hair. Six million people fucked a minute ago! I lowered my hair drying pink wand. I stared in the mirror. Probably close to 92 or 93 thousand people fucking every second. "I am definitely not oversexed."

I made up my mind to become a nymphomaniac right then and there. The only problem was approaching men. I already sold beauty products to women for a living. I can't say it's a boring job. It's just not fulfilling if you know what I mean.

But then a great idea occurred to me. All I needed to do is approach single men or male-only households!

I reprogrammed my computer matrix to search for single male households between the ages of twenty-three and thirty-five. Such a massive list repopulated my mailer program, I practically orgasmed!

The next day I wore a dark purple blouse, a blue and white striped tube skirt, my black pumps, and a big white grin. My long curly blonde hair gave me the excuse I needed. Blondes have more fun. I purrrrrrrrrrrrrrred.

I knocked on the expensive mahogany door. The knocker was shaped like some huge obscene object, a wooden peg, rounded on the holder's end. Soon a man opened the door. He wore a five- o'clock shadow.

"Is the Misses home? I'm selling beauty products."

"I'm sorry," the handsome hunk said, "I don't have a wife." He laughed. "Maybe we should go out together and change that?"

"Mmmm," I said. "Let me come in and show you what I'm selling." "If you insist." He let me ease by him.

As I passed him, I felt his groin rub ever so slightly against my hip. I wasn't disappointed or shocked. "Is it this way?" I pointed.

"Yes, the living room is on the left." His voice was deep and satisfying.

"Nice living room. Entertainment center. Yes, your Misses is going to love this house." "I built it myself. I'm a housing contractor."

"We have a lot in common. You build them, I sell inside them!" I wiggled my flat ass to make my point crystal clear.

· · ·

He cleared his deep voice, obviously unnerved by my sexuality. "I don't normally allow strangers in to sell beauty products."

"I promise you'll be a satisfied customer when I'm done." I parked my rolling attaché case. I removed the straps and opened the case. "First we have this shaving product."

"I could use a shave," The stranger said, rubbing his five-o'clock shadow.

I sprayed some women's shaving cream into my hand. "Now this smells flowery at first. Then it leaves a nice smell-free scent." I lathered up his chin. I told him to sit back. I straddled his blue jogging pants covered thighs. I took out my lady pink razor. I shaved his cheeks first.

The stranger relaxed and sank into his couch. His hips slid forward. His hard cock rocked against my clit as if it was a speed bump.

"No more sliding for now." I pressed down on his sweet hardness. When I finished shaving him, I took a towel and asked to see his bathroom. He smiled and pointed.

I went into his bathroom. I turned on the hot water and removed all my clothes. I got the towel nice and hot. I returned and the stranger contractor's jaw dropped.

"You're gorgeous. I wanted to see your petite vanilla legs and those melon tits on your chest." "You're seeing them." I cooed. "First let's take care of your shave."

I wrapped the hot white towel all over the stranger's face. He closed his eyes. "The steam feels good."

"This softens the hairs." While I left the towel on his face, I reached my hand under and removed his cock. He was thick as a healthy tree limb. "An instrument like this needs a cover." He groaned under the hot towel.

"Don't go to sleep under there!" I said stroking his wang tool up and down vigorously. I twisted my palm around the tip for special emphasis. He responded by lubing my hand with his clear precum.

He took a deep breath. "I couldn't sleep if I tried."

"Do you remember how I look?" I laughed as I pushed his cock under my skirt and up between my swollen fuck flaps.

"Yeah. Long platinum blonde hair to your ass. Five feet, four, your melons have puffy nipple tips. If I didn't know better, I'd say you are carrying around one gallon of milk per tit. And your thighs--they are thick. I can tell you love fucking cowgirl style."

"Damn!" I purred. "I want to fuck myself after that description."

He slowly removed the white towel and stared into my glazed-over blue eyes. He didn't believe I'd be dry humping his thick fuck meat between my sweaty cooze. I removed my hands from his groin and abs and placed them on his shoulders. I rose up and fed him my oversized melons. "I use to be a farm girl, but now I'm all city girl."

"I've built a few barns in my times, too." He managed to say between gobbling on my tit flesh. After he licked both boobs so my nipples peaked; I lowered myself and still embracing his shoulders, planted the wettest, sexiest French Kiss I knew how.

. . .

He nibbled on my lower lips, He practically sucked in my tongue a few times. I didn't mind. Then he went back to expertly kissing my upper lip.

I was ready, steamy, and insatiable. "Six million people fucked a second ago. We're going to be in that next six million groups," I said as I pushed his long slong dong up my sloppy slot and bore down. I kept pressing down further and further until at last he bumped into my cervix.

"You are warm and deep."

"I've been empty for too long. I need some sperm up my quim."

He humped up inside me. He reached behind and gripped my butt cheeks. He literally picked me up and down, slamming me on his fuck tool. I never felt so helpless and fulfilled as that stranger contractor built new spaces inside my pussy space. He redecorated my pussy ripples. He lay some of them flat. He raised others up. He made sure the baselines of my cunt flowed evenly with the walls of my dripping slit. All I needed inside was a new white coating of sperm on my juicy cunt walls.

He didn't disappoint.

He bounced my ass off his thighs faster than a jackhammer. I exploded, squirting all over him. Soon I was so dazed and satisfied; I came several times. He smiled as sweat dripped off his clean-shaven face. His dark hair coated his forehead. I rubbed my hands all over his clean face and sniffed my hand. I held them to his nose, as he kept tossing me like a fuckdoll all over his lap, reaching those delicious neglected spots inside my cunny crack. "See. No scent."

"I rather like the scent your pussy cave is emitting," he said bluntly and moaned as he blasted his white love paint up inside my squeezing cunt.

He apologized afterward for hitting my G-spot too many times. "I haven't fucked in a year. It was time to replenish my sperm stock."

I cooed. "I don't mind a little urgency. I'm trying to become the nymphomaniac myself. You want to help me?"

"I'll do my best."

"Good," I said raising off his drenched thighs and jogging pants. "When I get enough men together, I'll call you for the swing fest."

"I'll hold my natural white paint until you call."

"I reached inside my purse. "Cell number please."

CHAPTER 4

SPLENDID LOVE

PAUL WAS happy that he'd decided to do something special for his wife. After all, it was her birthday. When Candy found her husband in the kitchen, cooking her dinner, she'd been very impressed. She practically couldn't keep her hands off him since then. Had he known weeks ago, he would have cooked her dinner more often.

She looked amazing tonight in her tight-fitted dress. He'd followed her upstairs to their room, like a little puppy, desperate to get some attention. How his wife looked so good after over ten years of being together was beyond him. He was impressed. How did she keep her good looks?

Paul fixed his gaze directly on her and they sat for long moments looking into each other's eyes, then his gaze moved downwards to the top of her dress, then down further to her breast where his eyes lingered for long, insatiable moments. Candy felt him undressing her with his eyes and her breathing increased in pace and depth, she turned her head to one side and slowly used the very tip of her tongue to run along the side of his ear.

He brought his hand up to the back of her neck, where

he ran his fingers up and down, very, very slowly, causing goosebumps to rise on her lily-white skin. Then he ran his fingers through the back of her hair, and she gave a gasp as he gave a pull as he curled the hair in his fingers forming a fist. He pulled gently backward, exposing her neck, and placed his lips under her chin gently and with meaning. As her breathing deepened still further he nuzzled into her neck, and she began to feel a warm throbbing between her legs as her desire for him rose within her, she arched her back to accentuate the angle of her neck bending backward and brought her hand up from his inner thigh to rest between his legs.

Candy could feel his erection waiting for her, and once again she felt powerful, knowing that even after the way she had treated him today, he was still hot for her, he still wanted her, and probably always would. She pulled herself away from his and stood up before him, and then slowly removed her clothes, staring him in the eye all the time, daring him to reach out and touch her, but making it clear that that would not be allowed. Finally, she stood before him in her naked splendor; his eyes fixed on her as she brought her hand up by her shoulder and placed her fingers down.

Cupping her own breast she began using her fingertips to excite her own nipples. He gave out a groan and a sigh that seemed to last for centuries, as she ran her fingertips slowly down her own stomach, along the line of her groin, and down between her own legs to find her clit, hot, swollen, and ready. Paul shifted his position on the bed to be comfortable as his ever-growing erection throbbed between his legs, and she bit gently on her lower lip, lifting her eyebrows at him, daring him to reach out to touch her.

She rotated her whole pelvis as she ground against her

fingertips between her legs; she could feel her fingers growing wet against her pussy, and as her breathing became even deeper still, she curled her tongue out slightly towards him. She wondered if he was salivating as much as she was and if he was as hot for her as she was for him at that moment. This is where she wanted to be, with her husband - loyal, loving, and ready to fuck.

Paul could wait no longer, he seemed to spring from the bed and take hold of her, at the same time as dropping his trousers and pants, he tried to sling her sideways onto the bed as he strode out of the clothes fallen at his ankles, but Candy fell on her back looking up at him for one last second. And then he was on top of her, his hands everywhere her hands had just been, his whole mouth wrapped around her breast, cupping it from beneath as he used his lips to engulf her nipple.

As soon as his hands slipped onto her pussy he could feel she was ready for him. She was wet and swollen and raised her hips upwards into his groin, desperate for his erection, desperate to feel him inside her. He wasted no time, he placed his shaft long and deep inside her, lifted himself up on his muscular arms, and then bore down on her with a need that engulfed his whole being.

They moved in fluid movement together, as he drove fuller and deeper inside her, and she lost herself to the pleasures that racked her body. Her fingers slipped down between their legs, but rather than touching her clitoris, she pushed her fingertips into the very depth of his shaft, reaching up to his balls and massaging her fingertips deep into the soft flesh.

"I'm yours," Candy simply stated in his ear.

"Take me; take me now, harder Paul, harder. Take me with everything you've got, I will always be yours."

He exploded within her, his whole body engulfed in the rapture of his orgasm, as he continued to thrust ever more gently inside her.

As their bodies finally relaxed from the orgasms that had gripped them just a few minutes before, they once again met eyes. They lay together, locked together in their nakedness in a way they would not be able to lie together unless totally spent, and enjoyed each other's bodies. The curves, the smoothness of skin, the stretch, and the tone of muscle. Paul looked over at his wife she was beautiful. At that moment he believed that he must have been the luckiest man alive.

CHAPTER 5

THANKSGIVING AT THE BAR

"WHO SPENDS THANKSGIVING AT A BAR?" the young waitress asked with a huge smile on her gorgeous face.

"Me and you baby," Mack teased taking a gulp of the brandy he had in his glass. Ever since his wife Lucy left him, he'd become somewhat of a drunk spending all his time and money at the bar.

Mona must have been tired of seeing him hanging around the bar and although she didn't say anything or protest about it, Mack knew that she must have felt like he should be at home enjoying this holiday with his wife and two children.

Regardless, he knew Suzanna would not let him back into her life, so why bother going home, he thought to himself.

He other another round of drinks and gulped the strong alcohol down his throat without thinking twice. Mona had a weird look on her face but didn't say anything.

The bar was practically empty halfway during the evening. Since she owned the place, she decided to close early and call it a night. It was then the feeling of loneliness crept upon her. She was miles away from her family and had decided to keep the bar open, instead of traveling across the country to California to be with her parents on Thanksgiving.

The only person who seemed just as lonely as she was – was Mack Simmons. Mack seemed even lonelier than her. Poor guy, he'd told her his wife had left him and was filing for full custody of their two children.

She knew Mack, from his time at the bar, and he seemed like a genuinely nice guy. Why would a wife or a mother try to keep him from his children? He was one guy that should have been home with his family on Thanksgiving.

Mona walked up to him, to ask him if he needed her to call a cab or give him a ride to wherever he was staying. But surprisingly she realized that he was not as drunk as she'd thought while talking to him.

Soon their little chat turned into much more. They had locked lips in the process, and his tongue was feverishly exploring the inside of her mouth. As their passion increased, they began ripping away at each other clothes, until they were naked before each other.

Mona stood directly in front of him and pushed his back up against the bar, she licked her lips and slowly wrapped them around one of his nipples, where they lingered for what felt like an eternity. With the smallest of kisses, she moved to his mid-chest area, and then she started to trace her tongue downwards, further and further, kissing and nibbling all the way. He tipped his head back and gave out the greatest sigh as she reached the top of his pubic hair, she used her fingers to run through the hair and gently, gently pull as she continued to take her mouth down ever lower. Finally, her tongue traced around the end of his dick and she opened her mouth and wrapped her luscious lips around his dick, slowly pulling her mouth down around him, swallowing what felt like the entirety of his erection, then slipping her mouth back, with her tongue running along the underside of him.

Mack let out a moan like he had never experienced before, and she let her mouth slide off the end of him, while she continued to stroke his member with her fingertips, which felt like they must be on fire. She stood up, still wearing her waitress uniform, and dropped her pants to the floor. He undid her top button with care, but could no longer be patient and ripped at the further buttons, working them free one after the other until the front of her dress hung open, revealing tits that his groin ached for with desire. He spun her around so that it was now her turn to have her back against the bar and lifted her so that her pretty little ass was now propped on the edge. He buried his face deep within her tits, using both hands to squeeze them gently together and losing himself within them.

She laughed at him and pressed them together, leaning down and using her tongue to circle one of her nipples, and he joined her as the skin puckered and hardened beneath their mouths. Their mouths met time and again, but they never kissed; this was about pure sex, not love, and very soon he could wait no longer. He worked his hands down to find her wet and ready. She too was swollen and throbbing, as hungry for him as he was for her. He wasted no more time, taking his dick to her slit and thrusting up inside her. She gave out a moan and wrapped her legs firmly around his lower back, bracing herself as she perched right on the edge of the bar, opening herself to him as he thrust again and again.

He filled all of her and quickly he was deep, deep inside her rhythmic and frantic. She leaned back so that his pubes were rubbing on her clit, taking her higher and higher. He pounded faster and faster, seeing her leaning right back on the bar with her tits hanging out the front of her dress was too much for him and they both exploded at the same time. Over and over the moment took them as the rhythm slowed and came to a stop.

Within moments he realized what he had done, and was horrified by the way he had allowed himself to be seduced so easily and freely by this beautiful waitress. He looked at her and told himself that no man would be able to resist the temptation of a woman like this rubbing against him, but deep down he knew what he had done was wrong, and he wasn't sure where to put his eyes.

"I won't tell," she said, and he knew it was true, he knew that his moment of guilty pleasure would never be spoken of again, and would remain only in his fantasies until he could no longer remember if it was fantasy or not.

ABOUT THE AUTHOR

Shon Gacy is an emerging erotica author of many erotica kinks and sub-genres. Be sure to check out other books and leave a review if this story got you hot!

Visit my blog at Shon Gacy Blog

Join my newsletter for exclusive Shon Gacy Newsletter

Sign up for Free Stories from Xplicit Press Authors

Xplicit Press Author Updates

Like Xplicit Press on Facebook

Follow Xplicit Press on Twitter

Readers: I want to expand a few of the stories to see where the characters can be explored further. If there are any of the stories that you would like to read more about again, I'd love to hear from you!

Keep In Touch
Shon Gacy
info@shongacy.com